Contents

SHIMMERING
GLACIER

ROSE'S HOUSE

SNOWFLAKE
MOUNTAINS

POPPY'S
HOUSE

RAINBOW RIVER

OAKWINGS
ACADEMY

DANDELION
FIELDS

Chapter One

As the bluebell rang, Poppy Merrymoss leaped out of bed. Her wings buzzed with excitement and her tummy swirled with nerves as she realised what day it was.

"Wake up, Rose!" she called to her best friend. There was a flutter from the bed above. Rose hung upside down from the top bunk and squealed. "We're going to the Snowflake Mountains!"

As soon as Poppy saw Rose's huge grin, all of her nerves disappeared. She had been a bit scared about going on her very first school trip, but anywhere she went with her best friends Rose and Ninad was sure to be fun!

"I'm sooooooo excited!" Rose cried, whizzing around the room as her long braids whipped back and forth. She bumped the desk and sent a pile of books tumbling to the floor. "Whoops!"

Poppy giggled as she began filling her bag with everything she needed for the trip.

"You're going to need lots of warm layers," Rose told her.

Rose's family lived in the Snowflake Mountains. She was always telling Poppy how icy cold it was there, so Poppy packed her thickest lambswool jumper, woolly socks made from soft moss and a catkin scarf.

"Don't forget this," Rose said, handing Poppy a beautiful white coat that they'd been given on their first lesson with snow fairy Mr Winterwell. It was made from thick, fluffy swan feathers which were waterproof on the outside but toasty warm on the inside. Rose had one exactly the same. She hugged it tightly.

"Swan feathers are so cosy," she said, snuggling into it. "It's so kind of them to give us fairies their spare feathers."

Their other roommate, Celeste Greenshoot, snorted as she added to

the huge pile of clothes on her bed. "My coat is made from dandelion fluff, which is *much* warmer and cosier than swan feathers. And MUCH more expensive."

Rose rolled her eyes. "We're only supposed to bring *one* bag, Celeste," she told her.

Celeste already had two bags which were stuffed to bursting. She had started packing a third bag with no signs of stopping.

"I *need* all of these things," Celeste said. As usual, Celeste was dressed in the finest fairy clothes Poppy had ever seen. Her fancy dandelion coat looked softer than a newborn baby bunny's fur. Poppy had to resist the urge to stroke it.

"I've been to the Snowflake Mountains loads of times," Celeste said, pulling on a pair of pink peony-flower earmuffs. "My family go skiing there every year, so I'm practically an expert."

Rose huffed. "I think I know it better than you, Celeste," she said, crossing her arms. "As I actually *live* there!"

Celeste crinkled her nose at Rose then stuffed another fluffy jumper into her bag.

"Come on," Rose said, hooking her
arm in Poppy's. "It's almost time to go."

"I can't wait to see your home,"
Poppy said. "Will we meet your
mums?"

Rose's head drooped. "No, they've gone to help the fairies at the Whispering Waterfall," she said. "They were having a problem with icicles."

"Don't worry, I'll meet them next time!" Poppy said, giving her friend's arm a squeeze.

They gathered their belongings and fluttered down the twisty spiral staircase. It ran through the middle of the huge oak tree which was home to Oakwings Academy, the fairy forest school. They flew down to the entrance hall, looking for their friend Ninad as they went. "There he is!" Poppy said

as she saw him talking to a cute little
ladybird in the hallway.

"Spot! Stop climbing on me," Ninad
fussed as his pet
ladybird, Spot,
clambered over
his shoulders.
Ninad
laughed as
Spot tickled
his ear. He
lifted Spot and
carefully put
him on the
ground.

"He's a bit grumpy that I can't take him with us," Ninad said. "I've never been to the Snowflake Mountains before. I'm a bit worried about tobogganing — it sounds dangerous."

"You'll love it!" Rose said. "It's like flying, but faster and more fun."

"I haven't done it before either," Poppy said, smiling. "We can do it for the first time together."

But Ninad didn't smile back. He leaned in so that no one else could hear him. "I'm worried about Ms Webcap too," he admitted.

Ms Webcap was the deputy head

teacher, but she wasn't just a teacher —
Poppy and her friends had discovered
that she was secretly an evil fairy called
Lady Nightshade! Lady Nightshade
had cursed the fairy forest so that
no grown-up fairy would be able to
produce a magic seed. Magic seeds
usually appeared when fairies did an
especially helpful bit of magic, and the
fairies used them to make the fairy dust
that gave their wands magical powers.

Poppy gave Ninad a hug. "Don't
worry, Ms Webcap isn't coming,"
she said. "Mr Winterwell and Mrs
Sproutleaf are the teachers coming

with us. So it will be a break away from Lady Nightshade, as well as school."

That cheered Ninad up. "What are you looking forward to the most?" he asked.

"Everything!" Rose cried, flapping her wings. "I can't wait to go ice skating, and tobogganing, and make snowballs, and— oh! How could I forget the best part? The Winter Ball!"

Poppy and Ninad were still laughing at Rose's enthusiasm as Mr Winterwell flew into the Great Hall. He was very tall with snow-white hair and a long

white
beard
that hung
almost to
the floor.

"Gather around,
fairies," he called.
He held his wand
in one hand and a
magical map in the other.
But before he could use the map to
send them to the Snowflake Mountains,
Mr Winterwell frowned at something
behind them. Poppy turned to see Mrs
Sproutleaf flying towards them with her

arm in a leaf sling. She wore a daisy cap on her head and a flowy dress made from flower petals, but although her outfit was bright and cheerful, her face wasn't happy at all.

"What happened?"
Mr Winterwell
asked.

Mrs Sproutleaf
landed beside
him. "I got
bitten by a
snapdragon
flower. I can't
understand it,

Mr Winterwell, they're usually so calm and gentle."

"What about the trip, Mrs Sproutleaf?" Celeste called out. "Does this mean we can't go?"

"Celeste!" Poppy whispered. Celeste was always thinking about herself.

"What?" Celeste snapped. "I want to go on the trip."

Mrs Sproutleaf smiled at Celeste. "Luckily, another teacher has kindly agreed to take my place at the last minute."

She held her hand out to welcome her replacement.

Poppy's heart sank as she saw the teacher who would be coming with them. She wore a mushroom top skirt, and a short cape made from brown leaves. Spider webs shimmered in her long blonde hair. On her head sat a round, black hat, which Poppy knew was actually a spider called Webby. The teacher's mouth curled into a wicked smile as she flew past Poppy, Rose and Ninad.

"Oh no!" Poppy groaned. "It's Ms Webcap!"

Chapter Two

The Snowflake Mountains were just
as beautiful as Rose had promised.
The ground was covered in soft white,
powdery snow, making everything look
sparkly clean. Wooden log cabins stood
along a winding path at the edge of an
icy lake, their roofs topped with snow
like swirly, sugary frosting. It was truly
one of the most magical-looking places

Poppy had ever seen!

"If I lived here, I don't think I'd ever leave," Poppy told Rose. "It's wonderful!"

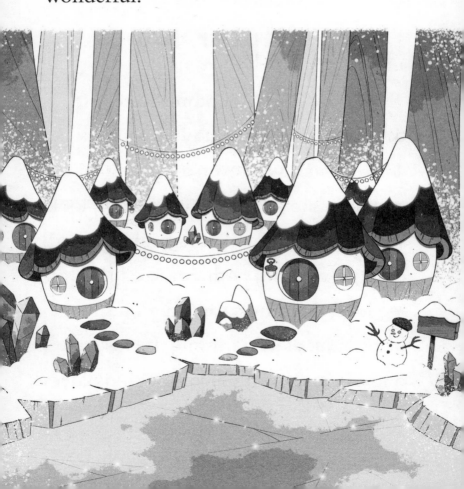

Rose beamed at Poppy proudly.

"Gather around," Mr Winterwell called. "Snow fairies live in log cabins like these. They work all over the mountains, making snow and ice, and helping all of the animals who live here." He held out his wand to demonstrate. With a quick swish and flick, a flurry of snow rose from the ground and swirled around the young fairies.

Rose clapped in delight, as Poppy watched on in awe.

Mr Winterwell smiled, then pointed his wand at a nearby pine tree. He whispered a spell and the snow resting along the branches began to melt. It dripped slowly down, before freezing into crystal-like icicles. The sunlight shone through them, casting glistening colours which danced around them.

"Wow!" gasped Ninad. "Can you show us how to do that?"

Mr Winterwell laughed. "One thing at a time," he said. "First, we need to unpack."

The class followed him along the path to a large log cabin. Inside was a huge fireplace with a warming fire crackling in the hearth. Dotted around

the room were plush comfy sofas and beanbags, and right in the middle was a long table and benches where they would eat.

Mr Winterwell told the boys to follow him down one corridor. The girls followed after Ms Webcap down another to their dorm rooms.

Instead of separate rooms, all the girls were sharing one large room. There were five bunk beds, and the fairies raced off to choose their beds.

Rose grabbed Poppy and dragged her to the closest one. "Poppy and I are sharing!" she shouted, plonking her bag down on the top bunk.

Poppy noticed that Celeste had taken the bed right next to the window. It had the best view of the mountains outside. Luckily, it was also the furthest bed away from Poppy and Rose.

"At least we won't have to listen to her showing off for once," Rose mumbled, giving Poppy a knowing look.

"Or her snoring!" Poppy giggled.

As soon as they had unpacked, Ms Webcap clapped her hands. "Put on your coats," she said sweetly, "We're going outside."

Poppy pulled on her swan-feather
coat and flew after the others back out
into the snow.

She pulled her
coat closer, glad
of the warmth.

The
Snowflake
Mountains
were beautiful
but Rose had
been right. It
was freezing!

Rose pointed to
the top of one of

the mountains. "Look!"

Snow fairies flew back and
forth, waving their wands over the
mountain. As they did so, flurries of
snow burst out of the sky, covering
the mountainside with a fresh layer.
Strange green, orange and purple lights
danced in the sky above and around
the snow fairies as they worked.

Some of the snow fairies were
working close by. Rose pulled Poppy
and Ninad over to take a closer look.

"What are you doing?" Rose asked
one of the snow fairies. She had a
swan-feather coat on and wore her

white hair in a long braid with a bright pink lambswool bobble hat on her head.

The fairy smiled at them kindly. "We are using the snowflake charm to make snow," she said. "So that the weather is perfect for animals like my friend Snowball here."

"Oh!" Ninad jumped in surprise as a furry white fox suddenly appeared by his side. The fox's thick fur was pure white and his eyes sparkled bright blue.

"He's so white I almost didn't spot him in the snow!" He laughed, and stroked the arctic fox's nose.

The snow fairy grinned. "Snowball

is very good at hide and seek," she said.

"I'm Alba Frostnip, nice to meet you."

Poppy shook Alba's hand. "I'm Poppy, and this is Rose and Ninad. We're visiting from Oakwings Academy."

"Have you found any magic seeds?" Rose asked Alba.

Alba shook her head sadly. "Since Lady Nightshade cast her evil spell, we haven't collected any magical seeds at all. Luckily, most of our snow magic comes from the snowflake charm."

At the mention of Lady Nightshade, Poppy glanced over at Ms Webcap. She knew that the curse had affected the forest around Oakwings Academy, but she didn't know it had travelled this far.

Alba smiled brightly at the fairies. "Would you like to see the snowflake charm?" she asked.

Rose's wings flapped excitedly. "Can we?!"

Alba nodded. She flew over to speak to Mr Winterwell, who nodded and gathered the rest of the class. They flew after Alba, chattering excitedly as she led them to the very top of the mountain. Finally she stopped in front of a large grey rock. Celeste elbowed her way to the front, but Alba held up her hands.

"The snowflake charm is very precious," she warned. "Please be careful not to touch it."

"We should make sure Ms Webcap doesn't go near it," Ninad whispered.

Poppy's tummy swirled. Ninad was right. Who knew what Ms Webcap – or rather, Lady Nightshade – would do with something as powerful as the snowflake charm. Poppy shuddered as she thought about the horrid fairy having all that power.

The crowd moved back and Poppy finally got a look at the charm. It was so dazzling she had to cover her eyes. It

was a solid crystal snowflake, as clear
as water. It reflected the light in all
directions as the sun shone down on
it, casting rainbows across the snowy
ground.

Celeste pushed her way to the front
again. As Alba told the fairies about

how the snowflake charm worked,
Rose winked at Poppy.

"I wonder what it feels like," Rose
said. "You should touch it and see,
Celeste."

Poppy looked at her friend in
confusion. *What was she up to?*

Celeste narrowed her eyes at Rose,
then looked at the snowflake charm.
Her eyes shone as she reached for the
snowflake. There was a sudden bright
blue flash as she touched it. Celeste
opened her mouth to scream, but no
sound came out because she had been
frozen solid, like a statue made of ice!

"Rose!" Ninad gasped. "What did you do?"

"She'll be fine," Rose said. "I'm sure she'll melt . . . sooner or later."

"Rose Seedpip!" Mr Winterwell shouted as he hurried over. "Your mums are snow fairies. You should know better!"

He waved his wand and Celeste instantly defrosted. She glared at Rose,

her eyes filled with rage, then stormed
off.

"Did you know that would happen?"
Poppy asked.

Rose smiled slyly. "Only snow fairies
can touch it because it is enchanted
by magic. You've seen what happens
if a non-snow fairy touches it," she
continued. "We have to look after it – it
would be a disaster if it was damaged
or destroyed."

As Rose talked, Poppy noticed a
shadow move behind her. She turned
quickly and saw a flash of blonde hair
and a glimpse of a black hat as Ms

Webcap hurried away.

"Do you think Ms Webcap heard us?" she whispered. "I have a horrible feeling that Ms Webcap might have put a spell on the snapdragon flower that bit Mrs Sproutleaf so that she could come here instead."

Poppy's skin turned to ice, but it wasn't because of the cold this time.

"What if she wanted to come here for a reason? Ms Webcap is planning to steal the snowflake charm!"

Chapter Three

Poppy placed the last block of snow on to her igloo.

"There!" she said, feeling proud of herself. She brushed the snow from her fluffy gloves and stepped back to admire her work.

After visiting the snowflake charm, the class had come back down the mountain and Mr Winterwell and the snow fairies had shown them how to make igloos. Every snow fairy had to learn how to make an igloo in case an animal friend needed to shelter. Poppy had been keeping a close eye on Ms Webcap but she hadn't turned into Lady Nightshade or done anything awful – yet!

Poppy was about to call Rose to show her the igloo, when it suddenly collapsed. The blocks of snow crumbled into a heap.

"Why won't it stay up!" Poppy grumbled.

Alba flew over to help.

"I've been using the ice block spell just like Mr Winterwell showed us," Poppy told her, "but my igloo keeps on collapsing!"

Alba smiled at Poppy kindly. "The ice block spell binds the snow together. But if it's not tightly packed enough, the snow crumbles. Watch me."

Alba gathered a big handful of snow. She squashed and squeezed it together into a rectangle then placed it on the ground. She pointed her wand at the block. "Fristy-frosty freeze!" she chanted.

The snow block slowly iced over until

it was almost see-through. Alba picked up the block and tapped it with her finger.

"See?" she said. "You have to make sure it is solid enough."

She put it down. "Now you try."

Poppy scooped up some snow, then narrowed her eyes in concentration.

"Fristy-frosty freeze!" she called out. The block turned to ice just as Alba's had.

"It worked!" she cried.

She made another, then another until she had a pile of ice blocks to rebuild her igloo.

"Thanks Alba!" Poppy beamed.

Together, they built the walls, stacking one block on top of the other. When the blocks ran out, Poppy used the ice spell to make more.

"We normally make igloos for animals if there's a blizzard," Alba said as they worked. "But recently it's been so hot that I've been making them for the arctic foxes just to keep them cool."

Snowball bounded around the igloo excitedly. "I think he likes this one!" Poppy giggled, flying out of reach as the cheeky arctic fox bent down and tried to lick her face. She snuggled into his warm fur and tickled his tummy.

"What are the snow fairies doing over there?" she asked Alba, pointing at the frozen lake at the bottom of the hill. There was a big group fluttering

around at the edge of the lake.

"They are making a giant igloo for the Winter Ball tomorrow night," Alba said.

Poppy felt a rush of excitement. She'd never been to a ball before, and she'd definitely never been to a ball on ice!

"Poppy!" Rose shouted, interrupting her daydream. "Mr Winterwell says it's time to go tobogganing!"

Poppy's excitement burst into a flurry of nerves. She followed Rose to a worn path at the base of the mountain. They each collected a wooden toboggan at the bottom.

"It's very high up," Ninad puffed as he pulled his toboggan along behind Poppy and Rose. "It would be so much easier if we could fly!"

Poppy agreed, but the toboggans were too heavy to lift into the air.

When they finally reached the top, they lined their toboggans up next to each other in a row.

"Ready?" Rose asked.

Poppy nodded but Ninad's hands shook and his face had turned a little bit green.

"Race you!" Rose said, kicking off. She zoomed down the mountain,

whooping and laughing the
whole
way.

Poppy
held on
tightly to
the twine at
the front of
the toboggan.
"We can do it,
Ninad," she said. "Let's go at the same
time." Ninad nodded and Poppy gave
him a reassuring smile. "One, two,
three . . ."

She pushed off her toboggan, racing

down the mountain so fast that everything was a big white blur around her.

Ninad quickly caught up with her. "This is so much fun!" he yelled.

When her toboggan came to a stop, Poppy jumped off, her legs feeling shaky and her heart pounding. "That was brilliant!" she cried.

"I told you you'd love it!" Rose said, squeezing Poppy into a hug.

"Gather round, class!" Mr Winterwell called them over to where Alba and Snowball were waiting.

"Snowball is going to demonstrate his

amazing tracking skills," Alba said. "I have hidden my glove somewhere on the mountain." She wiggled her bare fingers. "Let's see how quickly Snowball can sniff it out."

Snowball raced off, kicking up snow in all directions. He bounded up the mountain, sniffing at the ground as though he was following an invisible trail. Then he let out a loud howl and dug at a spot in the snow. He pulled out the fluffy pink glove between his jaws triumphantly. Poppy and the other fairies clapped and cheered.

Snowball returned the glove to Alba

and grinned proudly.

"Snowball's tracking is a very useful skill," Alba told them. "If anyone ever gets lost in the mountains, all he needs is something with their scent to find them." She stroked Snowball's side and smiled proudly. "Now, I think there's time for one more toboggan ride before dinner."

"Yes!" Rose shouted, jumping in the air. "How about another race, Ninad? Winner gets the biggest marshmallow in their hot chocolate!"

Before Ninad could answer, the ground beneath them trembled.

Poppy grabbed on to Rose. "What's happening?"

"Avalanche!" the snow fairies warned.

"Fairies, follow me!" Mr Winterwell ordered.

They flew down the mountainside as the rumbles grew louder.

In front of them, Celeste stopped as her peony earmuffs were blown off by the swirling wind. "My earmuffs!" she cried.

She turned and flew past Poppy, heading back up the mountain.

"Celeste, no!" Poppy called out. "It's not safe!"

"I need my earmuffs!" Celeste snapped back, a determined look on her face. "They were VERY expensive!"

Poppy watched the class disappear down the mountain. Then she took a deep breath and flew after Celeste.

At the top of the mountain, snow had started to move, like water flowing down a hill. Celeste was searching the snow for her earmuffs. But the snow was sliding down right above her!

"Celeste!" Poppy yelled. But Celeste couldn't hear her over the rumbling sound.

Poppy put on an extra burst of speed and grabbed Celeste, pulling her out of the way just as a tidal wave of snow thundered right over where Celeste had been searching. Celeste stared at Poppy, breathing fast. It was the first time Poppy had ever seen Celeste speechless.

"That was close!" Poppy gasped. "We have to get off this mountain!"

They flew quickly to the safety of their cabin where the other fairies were huddled, trying to get warm.

"Poppy!" Rose called, rushing to give Poppy a hug. "I was so worried, where were you?"

"Saving Celeste," Poppy said. "She needed her earmuffs."

Rose put her hands on her hips and glared at Celeste. "That was so dangerous!"

Celeste narrowed her eyes at Rose. Her hands were shaking, but she didn't reply. She flew off to their room.

"So rude!" Rose huffed. "And she didn't even say thank you."

Mr Winterwell counted the fairies to make sure that everyone was safe.

"Where's Ms Webcap?" Ninad muttered.

Poppy looked around, but the teacher

was nowhere to be found.

"Wherever she is, I bet she's up to something," Poppy said, "we should—"

She was interrupted by loud shouts outside.

"What's going on?" Poppy asked.

She flew to the window. The snow fairies were frantically searching the mountain for something. They flew back and forth, calling out to each other with panicked looks on their faces. Then Poppy heard what they were saying.

"The snowflake charm is missing!"

Chapter Four

The young fairies sat inside the cabin, whispering among themselves about what could have happened to the snowflake charm. All of the excitement from the tobogganing had gone.

"I'll make us some hot chocolate," Mr Winterwell said. "We've all had a bit of a shock."

He waved his wand and steaming

acorn cups filled with delicious hot chocolate appeared in front of each fairy, complete with a huge swirl of whipped cream and marshmallows on top.

Poppy held her cup to warm her hands but her tummy was too nervous to drink any. She flew over to the window and Rose and Ninad joined her. They looked out into the mountains where snow fairies flew back and forth, searching for any signs of the charm.

"Do you think Lady Nightshade had anything to do with this?" Ninad asked.

Rose nodded. "Of course she did!"

Poppy understood why Rose was so
angry. The Snowflake Mountains were
her home, and the snow fairies were
her family. The snowflake charm was
important for them to do their magic.
Otherwise . . . Poppy couldn't bear to
think about what might happen now
that the magic had gone.

A sudden horrible thought came

to her. "What if Lady Nightshade started the avalanche?" she hissed. "She couldn't touch the charm, but she could have used the avalanche to knock it off!"

Ninad's face turned white. "But . . . someone could have been really hurt!" he stammered.

The door to the cabin flew open and Alba appeared in the doorway. Her cheerful smile had gone and she frowned as she spoke to Mr Winterwell.

"What's going on?" Poppy asked, hurrying over.

Alba gave Poppy a small smile. "I'm

arranging a search party," she said.
"The Snowflake Charm might be
buried deep beneath the snow. We need
all the help we
can get to
find it."

"I want to
help!" Poppy
said.

"Us too!"
Rose and
Ninad said
together.

Mr
Winterwell

quickly organised them into a search party and they followed Alba out on to the mountain. The air was a lot colder now that the sun was setting. The fresh snowfall had covered all of their tracks from tobogganing, and the igloos they had made had been flattened by the avalanche. Everything was deadly quiet, like all the fun and laughter had been buried under the snow too. They each took a different section of the mountain, flying back and forth to see if they could spot any sign of the missing charm. Below her, Poppy could see Snowball along with more arctic

foxes digging in the snow.

"We have to find it, Poppy!" Rose
sniffled.

Poppy hugged her friend. "We will,"
she said, determined not to let Lady
Nightshade win.

There was a loud cry from the air,
and they both looked to the sky.

"It's L-L-Lady N-N-Nightshade!"
Ninad shrieked.

The fairies and foxes on the
mountain all looked up. Lady
Nightshade swooped overhead, riding
on the back of a huge snowy owl. Her
long cloak flapped behind her. Only

Poppy, Rose and Ninad knew who she really was. They had tried to tell their teachers at Oakwings, but tricky Ms Webcap had made sure nobody believed them.

The owl let out an ear-piercing screech. Its long, sharp talons curled beneath its body as it flew overhead.

"You'll never find the snowflake charm!" Lady Nightshade shrieked. "The avalanche was the perfect distraction! My owl has hidden it where no fairy will ever find it!"

She cackled with glee and the owl swooped close to the ground. She

scooped up some snow and her pet
spider, Webby, pelted hard snowballs at
the fairies before she flew away.

"We can't let her get away with

this!" Poppy cried. "I'm going to tell Mr Winterwell the truth about Lady Nightshade and this time I'll make him believe me!"

She clenched her fists tight and scanned the mountain until she spotted his long white beard.

"Mr Winterwell!" she called, hurrying towards him.

But before she could reach him, Ms Webcap appeared from out of nowhere, looking like an ordinary teacher again. Her spider pet was now sitting still and silent on the top of her head, pretending to be a hat.

"Just where do you think you are going?" Ms Webcap asked, putting her hands on her hips.

Poppy scowled. "To tell Mr Winterwell the truth about you being Lady Nightshade and stealing the snowflake charm!"

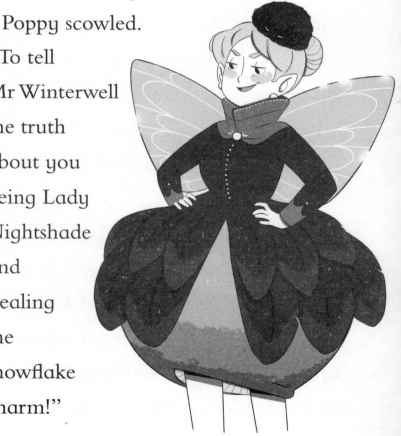

Ms Webcap's lip curled as she gave Poppy an evil smile. "He won't believe you." She grinned wickedly. "After all, I've been out searching for it, I'm SO concerned about the poor snow fairies and their precious charm."

"He will! He . . ." Poppy started.

"No one else has believed you," Ms Webcap continued.

Poppy felt all the fight go out of her. Ms Webcap was right. Even her Aunt Lily, who was a teacher at Oakwings Academy, hadn't believed her when she'd tried to tell her the truth. Why would Mr Winterwell be any different?

Ms Webcap winked at Poppy, then joined Mr Winterwell. They whispered for a minute, then Mr Winterwell nodded.

"Students, gather round," Mr Winterwell called. "It's getting dark and it's too dangerous for young fairies out here. You are to return to the cabin with Ms Webcap."

"Wait!" Poppy called as Mr Winterwell flew off. But she was too late. He was already halfway up the mountain.

Ms Webcap narrowed her eyes at Poppy as she led them back into the cabin. "Come along, Miss Merrymoss," she said, her voice sickly sweet. "There's absolutely *nothing* you can do."

Chapter Five

Poppy stared glumly out of the window.
She wished she was out there looking
for the snowflake charm.

"I've had an idea," Ninad whispered.
He glanced around to make sure none
of the other fairies were listening.
Especially Ms Webcap. She seemed to
be busy listening to Celeste chattering
on, but she kept on shooting suspicious

glances their way. "What if the reason the snow fairies can't find the snowflake charm out on the mountain is because it isn't there?"

Poppy frowned. "What do you mean?"

Ninad moved closer and paused as Ms Webcap glared at them again, then he continued quietly, "Wouldn't Lady Nightshade want to keep the snowflake charm somewhere nearby, in case she needed to escape with it quickly?"

Poppy's eyes grew wide. "Somewhere like this cabin!" she squealed.

Beside her, Rose's wings buzzed with

excitement. "You're a genius, Ninad!"

Trying to not look too suspicious, the three friends split up. Ninad searched the boys' dorm room while Rose checked the girls'. Poppy stayed in the main room, peeping under cushions and behind shelves for any sign of the snowflake charm. But the cabin wasn't very big and it wasn't long before Ninad and Rose returned.

"Anything?" Poppy asked.

Ninad and Rose both shook their heads.

Poppy let out a loud sigh. "It has to be somewhere!" she huffed.

She glanced out of the window again.
The snow fairies were still searching.
Now that it was darker, small lights
from their wands flickered to and fro as
they flew. Poppy looked at the icy lake
where the huge igloo stood, ready for
the Winter Ball that might not happen
now that the charm was gone.

A dark shadow moved across the lake's surface. The snowy owl that Lady Nightshade had ridden on earlier was swooping back and forth. It circled high above the lake as though it was looking for something. *Or*, Poppy gasped, *guarding something…*

"The lake!" she hissed. "The

snowflake charm is in the lake!"

Ninad glanced nervously at Ms Webcap, who was looking bored as Celeste continued chatting non-stop at her. "How are we going to get outside without Ms Webcap noticing?"

Rose's eyes lit up. "Leave that to me."

She disappeared for a few moments, then returned with a shocked look on her face, flying right for Celeste.

"Celeste! Come quickly!" she shouted. "*Someone* left the window open in our dorm. The icicles have melted all over your beautiful clothes!"

Celeste leaped into the air with an

ear-piercing shriek!

"No, no, no!" she screamed. "Not my clothes! Someone, help me!"

Ms Webcap rolled her eyes and followed after Celeste. Rose turned to Poppy and Ninad and gave them a thumbs up.

"Let's get out of here!" she said.

They sneaked out of the cabin while everyone was distracted by Celeste's wails, and flew down to the edge of the icy lake. Poppy scanned the sky for any sign of the snowy owl, but it seemed to have gone, for now.

Ninad's face fell as he stared at the

icy lake. "It's huge!" he said.

"How are we going to find the
snowflake charm in this?" Poppy
sighed.

Rose held up a finger. "Lady
Nightshade said that she'd hidden the
charm where no *fairy* could find it. But
what if someone or *something* else could
reach it? Something like an arctic fox?"

"Snowball!" Ninad cried. "We can
use his amazing tracking skills."

Poppy nodded. "We could give him
something of Ms Webcap's and he
could sniff out the charm!"

Rose raced back to the cabin and

sneaked back inside. She was
back in a flash, hiding something
beneath her swan-feather coat.

She pulled Poppy and
Ninad behind a tall pine
tree to show them what she
was hiding.

"Ms Webcap's leaf
cape!" she said.

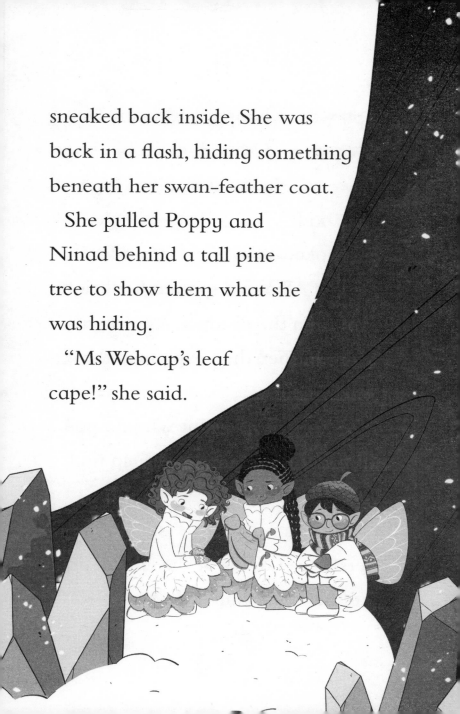

Poppy was so happy she laughed, and pulled Rose and Ninad into a big hug. "You two are the most brilliant friends I've ever had!"

They looked on the mountain for any sign of Alba and spotted her bright bobble hat in the distance. As soon as they reached her, they explained the plan.

"Hmm," Alba said. "But why do you think Ms Webcap's cape can help find the snowflake charm?"

"It's because . . . umm . . . she was the last person we saw near the charm and some of her scent might have rubbed

off?" Poppy said, hoping Alba would believe her.

Alba frowned, but seeing the fairies' hopeful faces she sighed. "OK," she said. "You can borrow Snowball. But I'm going to continue searching the mountainside."

Poppy hugged Alba. "Thank you!" she cried.

Ninad whistled and Snowball bounded towards them. He licked each of their faces in turn, leaving big slobbery trails.

Poppy wiped her face then held out the leaf cape. "Do you think you can

find something that smells like this?"
she asked.

Snowball gave the cape a big sniff,
then he nodded his head and ran off.

"Wait for us!" Poppy called.

They flew as fast as they could, but
Snowball was faster. He didn't slip
or slide across the icy surface once
thanks to his sharp claws. When he was
almost at the very centre of the lake, he
skidded to a stop and growled.

The fairies caught up and landed
beside him. They peered through the
crystal-clear ice. Right beneath them,
sparkling blue and silver, was the

snowflake charm!

"You found it!" Ninad said, patting
Snowball's fluffy head.

Poppy inspected the ice. It was so

thick that there was no chance of the ice cracking and them falling in. But then she realised that meant something else too.

"How are we going to get it out of there?"

Chapter Six

The lake's icy surface was frozen solid, and thicker than a tree trunk.

Rose had found a stick nearby and was using it to stab at the ice, but it wasn't really working.

"There must be a better way to get through it," Poppy huffed.

Rose dropped the stick. "I know! It will take us for ever with a stick."

"Maybe we could use a spell?" suggested Ninad.

Poppy's eyes lit up as she had an idea. "What if we use the ice block spell, but change it so that instead of the ice getting harder, it melts?"

Ninad brushed his messy hair from his eyes. "It could work," he said.

Poppy held out her wand and repeated the ice block spell. "Fristy-frosty UN-freeze!" she cried.

A small pink spark flew from the end of her wand and hit the ice.

Poppy paused. "That didn't happen the last time I used this spell," she said.

But when she looked closer, the spark had made a small crack in the frozen surface.

"It worked!" Rose said, doing a loop-the-loop.

"Try again!" Ninad said.

Poppy did the spell again and the ice broke a little more. Then Ninad and Rose joined in. Slowly, the magic from the spell chipped away at the ice, layer by layer, getting closer and closer to the snowflake charm.

"We're almost there!" Rose squealed excitedly. She reached down into the crack. "I think I can . . ."

"Uh . . . Poppy," Ninad whispered.
His arm shook as he pointed to the sky.
"Is that . . .?"

"Lady Nightshade!" Poppy cried as
the owl flew towards them. "We have to
get the charm before she does!"

There was a loud screech as Lady
Nightshade swooped towards them on
the back of the snowy owl. She pointed
her magic toadstool at Snowball,
whispering a spell under her breath.
Then she gave Poppy an evil smile.
"Get them!"

Snowball's eyes turned completely
black. He prowled towards Poppy and

her friends, growling.

Ninad backed away. "Snowball! It's us, your friends, remember?"

But Snowball was under Lady

Nightshade's spell! He reared forward and pounced at Ninad, almost catching Ninad's wing in his sharp teeth.

"Fly!" Poppy shouted.

They flew into the air as Snowball chased after them. He jumped, snapping his jaws and growling.

"Lady Nightshade is going after the charm!" Poppy cried. "We can't let her get it!"

Lady Nightshade was closing in on the snowflake charm. Poppy raced after her, but in one swoop, Lady Nightshade's owl swept down and plucked the charm from the ice as

Poppy looked on in horror.

There was a loud growl behind Poppy, and Rose screamed a warning. Poppy shot into the air just in time to avoid being eaten by Snowball. She tried to out-fly him, but he was fast. She zipped one way and he followed, his jaws getting closer as she became more tired. She zipped a different way, but Snowball followed her every move.

"We have to split up," Poppy shouted to her friends. "Snowball can't chase all of us if we fly in different directions."

Rose and Ninad flew to get Snowball's attention before heading in different directions.

Snowball paused, confused. He watched Poppy and Rose, then he took off across the ice after Ninad who was the slowest.

"Go and get the charm back!" Ninad shouted. He yelped as Snowball snapped his jaws at his feet.

Poppy and Rose flew after Lady Nightshade. Poppy almost caught up, but the owl dipped its powerful wings and dived out of the way.

The owl was fast, but Rose was even faster. Her wings buzzed, moving twice as fast as the owl's. She quickly caught

up, and reached for the snowflake
charm dangling from the owl's talon's
but missed it at the last second.

"Fly faster, you useless creature!"

Lady Nightshade screamed at the owl.
She dug her feet into its feathery sides
and the owl squawked.

Lady Nightshade turned and held out

her toadstool wand, pointing it at the girls. Bright flashes of lightning shot out of it. Poppy dodged to one side as the bolt zipped past her, smashing down into the icy lake below. There was a loud explosion, and the ice opened like a long scar, carving a deep crevasse in the ice. Lady Nightshade shot more lightning bolts at Poppy and Rose. They zoomed up and down, left and right, trying to not get hit.

Suddenly, there was a shout from below. Ninad had stopped at the edge of the crack and was waving at Poppy wildly. He pointed at the large crack in the ice. "Snowball has fallen in. We have to save him!"

Chapter Seven

Lady Nightshade cackled as she flew away from the lake, her owl still clutching the snowflake charm.

"She's getting away!" Rose cried.

Poppy watched Lady Nightshade then looked down at Ninad and Snowball. "We have to help Snowball," she decided. "It's not his fault that Lady Nightshade put a spell on him."

Rose nodded in agreement. "But what about the charm?"

"We'll help Snowball first and then go after Lady Nightshade," Poppy said.

They flew down to the lake. Snowball was whimpering as Ninad tried to keep him calm. The arctic fox clung on to the edge of the ice with his claws.

But he was slowly slipping further and further into the water.

Poppy held on to one of his front paws, clinging on to his fur so that he wouldn't slip any further. Rose held on to his other paw and Ninad flew behind Snowball to push him from the back.

"We're going to have to work together to pull him out," Poppy called.

Holding on to Snowball as tightly as they could, they flapped their wings and pulled and strained with all their might. But Snowball was so heavy and they were only three small fairies. They flapped and pulled and huffed and puffed, but Snowball didn't move an inch. Then he started to slip backwards, until his claws were barely clinging on to the edge.

"Pull!" Poppy cried. Her wings felt so heavy she could hardly move them, but she wouldn't let go. Then, just as it seemed that all was lost, Snowball's eyes changed from black to light blue again. Lady Nightshade's spell had worn off!

He dug his claws into the ice harder and with the fairies' help, slowly crawled, bit by bit, out of the lake.

When he was safe, he licked each of them them in turn, covering them in sticky slobber. "Ew, Snowball!" Rose squealed, pushing him off.

Ninad, who usually loved playing with animals, seemed distracted as he stared at the ice.

Poppy wiped the slobber from her wings and looked to the sky. "Now for Lady Nightshade," she said. "Let's get that snowflake charm back to where it belongs."

Ninad and Rose followed, with Snowball racing along below.

It wasn't long before Poppy spotted

the snowy owl perched on a pine tree. Lady Nightshade was shouting and pulling at his feathers, but the tired owl was panting with exhaustion.

Lady Nightshade spotted them and gave a wail of frustration. "Go, you lazy featherbrain!" she cried, kicking her legs into the owl's side again.

The owl squawked, turning its head to peck at Lady Nightshade's arm.

"Owwwww!" she screeched, pulling hard on the owl's feathers. The owl turned its head all the way round to give her a cross look, then dropped the snowflake charm.

"I'll get it!" Rose shouted, zooming forward in a blur.

"You can't touch it, you'll turn to ice!" Poppy warned her.

"I don't care! Lady Nightshade can't have it!" Rose sped up.

Poppy held her breath as Rose darted forward. Rose twisted in the air, doing a triple somersault, and caught the charm in one hand.

Poppy could hardly bear to look. What if her friend turned to ice as she flew and smashed on the ground below?

But then she heard a familiar sound

– Rose was laughing! Poppy opened her eyes to see Rose whooping with delight and doing loops, holding the snowflake charm.

Poppy grinned at her friend as she flew up to them. "You did it, Rose!"

"Does this mean you're a snow fairy?" Ninad asked.

The owl gave a loud, angry *HOOT!* before disappearing into the mountains. Lady Nightshade held on to her injured arm as she glared at the young fairies. "You were lucky this time," she scowled. "But you won't stop me!" She waved her magic toadstool and disappeared.

Poppy and her friends flew back to the far side of the lake, back to the cabins. Rose held up the snowflake charm in triumph.

"You were amazing, Rose!" Ninad said.

"You really were," Poppy agreed. "You saved the day! And I guess we

know what kind of fairy you'll be
when you grow up!"

"I guess so!" Rose grinned.

The friends hugged and jumped up
and down in celebration.

"Ow!" Rose grumbled. "What are
you holding, Ninad? It's jabbing into
me."

Ninad turned pink, then his eyes
grew wide. "I almost forgot!"

He reached beneath his wing and
pulled out something silver and shiny.

Rose's jaw dropped. "Is that . . .?"

"A magic seed!" Poppy finished.

Ninad, brushed his hair out of his

eyes and gave a small smile. "After we pulled Snowball out of the ice, I noticed something shining in the ice. I reached down and there it was."

"It must have appeared when we helped Snowball!" Rose said.

"Wait until Aunt Lily hears about this!" Poppy cried excitedly. Her aunt was a teacher at Oakwings Academy. She planted the magic seeds in the school's greenhouse and helped them to grow so that the fairies could use their magic dust.

"Let's go and find Mr Winterwell and the snow fairies before Lady

Nightshade or Ms Webcap return,"
Ninad said, biting his lip nervously.

Poppy couldn't believe that they had produced another magic seed by doing a good deed. *Maybe Lady Nightshade's curse isn't as powerful as she thinks it is*, Poppy thought to herself with a smile.

"Let's find Alba and get the snowflake charm back where it belongs!" she said.

Chapter Eight

They didn't need to look for Alba for long – Snowball led them straight to her, racing up to her so excitedly that he almost knocked her over.

"Snowball!" Alba laughed. "What has got into you?"

Snowball grinned and looked to Rose.

"Snowball helped us to find

something that you might want back,"
Rose said. She pulled the snowflake
charm from behind her back and held
it up for Alba to see.

Alba looked at each of the young
fairies in turn and shook her head.
"You found it! I can't believe it! I can't
thank you enough."

"We couldn't have done it without
Snowball," Poppy said.

Snowball nudged Alba with his nose
and she laughed, patting his head.
"Thank you too, Snowball."

She took the charm from Rose. "I'd
better get this back on the mountain,"

she said giving them each a hug.
"Thank you! We will make sure that it
is extra protected from now on."

Rose wiped away a happy tear and
Poppy pulled her and Ninad in for
another hug.

"Now for the seed," Poppy said.

They headed back to the cabin to find Mr Winterwell. Inside, the old teacher was trying to calm down a shrieking Celeste. As soon as she saw them, Celeste jabbed her finger at Rose.

"It was all *her* fault, Mr Winterwell!" Celeste screeched, holding up a dripping-wet dandelion fluff coat.

Rose tried to cover her grin as Mr Winterwell narrowed his eyes at her.

"Where have you three been?" he asked slowly.

"We are going to be in so much

trouble," Ninad muttered beneath his breath.

"Yes!" Celeste shrieked. "Where have you been? You ruined my beautiful coat and then sneaked out, even though Mr Winterwell told us to stay here. You should have them expelled from Oakwings Academy!"

She folded her arms and glared at Poppy and her friends.

Mr Winterwell frowned. "Poppy?" he asked.

Poppy nudged Ninad forward. "Show him the seed," she hissed.

"Oh, I . . .we . . .we helped to save Snowball from the ice, and also we found the snowflake charm and this," he stuttered.

He held out his hand to show everyone the shiny seed.

Mr Winterwell took the seed from Ninad and broke into a huge grin. "This is wonderful!" he said. "We must give this to Ms Mayblossom right away, she will be so pleased. Did you really find the snowflake charm too?"

Rose nodded, then poked her tongue out at Celeste, who turned so red Poppy thought she might explode.

"I'm going to take this back to Ms Mayblossom in the greenhouse right away," he said, pulling out his wand and magic map.

"But what about my wet clothes?"
Celeste grumbled.

Mr Winterwell sighed. "They will dry
off, Celeste. Go and hang them up."

He was holding up the map when
the cabin door slammed open, startling
them. A tall, dark shadow loomed in
the doorway.

"Ms Webcap!" Ninad squeaked.

Poppy moved closer to Ninad and
Rose, standing firm. She looked Ms
Webcap right in the eyes. She wasn't
going to be afraid of her any more.

"Oh dear, Ms Webcap. What
happened?" Mr Winterwell asked.

Ms Webcap held her arm close to her chest. She had wrapped it in a long fern leaf to make an arm sling.

She glanced at Poppy then put on a fake smile. "I just popped outside for some firewood and slipped on the ice," she said.

"That's not true!" Poppy said. "She tried to stop us from finding the snowflake charm that *she* stole!"

Mr Winterwell looked confused. "Why didn't you fly?" he asked. "That would have been much safer than walking."

Ms Webcap's eyes darted to and fro as though looking for a good lie. Then she smiled her wicked grin again and opened her hand. Inside was a pile of grey powder. She blew it into Mr Winterwell's face and he coughed. Then his eyes glazed over.

"Powdered fungus," she told Poppy who stared at Mr Winterwell in horror. "Alters the memory. Sadly it only works on adult fairies, or I'd wipe your

memories cleaner than the snow out there!"

Mr Winterwell coughed again and seemed to come out of his trance.

"Ah, Ms Webcap," he said, smiling at Poppy, Rose and Ninad proudly. "Did you hear the good news? These three young fairies found the snowflake charm! Isn't that wonderful?"

"Yes. Wonderful," Ms Webcap said, gritting her teeth.

Poppy narrowed her eyes. The evil fairy had made Mr Winterwell forget, but at least they knew the truth about what had really happened to Ms

Webcap . . . or *Lady Nightshade*.

"You'd better go back to Oakwings and see Dr Petalpill," Mr Winterwell said. "All of my helpers seem to be getting injured lately! I'll come with you as I'm taking this new seed to Ms Mayblossom."

Ms Webcap's face turned to thunder as she saw the magic seed. But before she could say anything Mr Winterwell had tapped the magic map and they both disappeared in a swirl of lights.

Alba and the snow fairies came to the cabin while the teachers were away.

"We can't thank you enough," one

of the snow fairies said to Poppy, Rose
and Ninad.

Alba smiled. "Who knows what
might have happened if the charm had
been lost for ever."

Rose ran to look out of the window
as colourful lights appeared around the
mountains.

"Time to celebrate!" she shouted.

The snow fairies led the class out to
the huge igloo on the lake. Although
it was cold outside, inside it was cosy
and warm. Colourful lights twinkled on
the ceilings like stars. The snow fairies
danced and twirled across a crystal

floor in time to the music.

Poppy helped herself to a cup of steaming hot chocolate. It was thick and delicious and she dipped a sweet churro into it. Ninad was licking away at a green and purple frosty snow cone. Beside her, Rose slurped down a snowberry slushy. "Ouch!" she cried. "Brain freeze!"

"Call yourself a snow fairy?" Poppy teased.

"Come outside!" Alba called.

They followed her out where more snow fairies skated over the ice. They spun and leaped and laughed. Poppy

and her friends put on some skates.
They held on to each other as they
tried not to slip and fall over. Clumsy

Rose was surprisingly good and Ninad even managed to do a small spin without falling.

Poppy smiled as she watched her friends. She knew that Ms Webcap would be up to her horrible tricks again sooner or later, but for now they had won. The snowflake charm was safe, they had found another magic seed. And best of all, she was at the Winter Ball, skating with her very best friends in the world.

The End

Poppy and her friends are competing in the Lily Pad Lake Swimming Gala! They love learning to swim and spending time with their new froggy friends. But when Lady Nightshade fills the lake with thick algae, it's up to Poppy, Rose and Ninad to clean it up in time to save the gala and the tadpoles trapped beneath it!

Find out what happens in:
Lily Pad Rescue

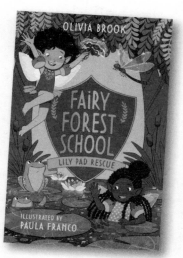

When Lady Nightshade puts a curse on the forest, covering it in smelly knotweed, Poppy and her friends rush to clear it up. But when they find a lost baby red panda amongst the knotweed, they must help him get home and save the forest. But the red panda only speaks in riddles! Can they solve the riddles before the forest is destroyed?

Find out what happens in:
Red Panda Riddle